I CAN'T TALK ABOUT IT

A book about sexual abuse
and healing
and learning to trust again.

©1986 by Multnomah Press
Portland, Oregon 97266
Printed in Hong Kong
All Rights reserved.
91   10 9 8 7 6 5 4
ISBN 0-88070-149-8

Sanford, Doris.
   I can't talk about it.
   Summary: At her grandmother's beach cot-
tage, Annie reveals her father's sexual abuse
of her to a dove who helps her heal and learn
to trust again. Lists guidelines for adults to
help sexually abused children.
   [1. Child molesting—Fiction. 2. Incest—
Fiction]
I. Evans, Graci, Ill. II. Title.
PZ7.S22495Ic 1986   [Fic]   86-831
ISBN 0-88070-149-8

the story by
Doris Sanford
and pictures by
Graci Evans

To the child who hasn't told . . .

yet.

". . . and the spirit of GOD came down from heaven like a DOVE."

from the Bible

Annie didn't know what to call him
but decided LOVE-DOVE was best.
Sometimes it was easier to call him LOVE for short.
Besides she wasn't sure if he was a dove.
It didn't matter really.
She knew he was her friend,
and Annie needed a friend *very* much!

Annie loved family vacations at Grandma's beach cottage.
And she loved low tide best of all.
Everything that had been covered up was open to see.

But this morning Annie was crying
and LOVE hopped over close
and cocked his head
so he could hear every word.

Annie said,
    "I don't like my daddy sometimes."

And LOVE said,
    "Tell me about that."

And Annie said, "*I CAN'T TELL.*
Daddy said if I tell
he won't love me anymore
and he will lock me up in the darkest corner
and Mommy will leave if she finds out."

Annie felt like throwing up just telling *that* much!
But LOVE looked kind,
so she continued.

"It all started three years ago.
Daddy brought me special toys
that he gave me when I went to bed.
Then he lay down with me.
At first I liked it.

"Before long though, I was *very* mixed up."

"When I told Daddy
I didn't like him touching my private parts,
he said,

       'You made this happen.
       You're causing it.
       And besides, you really like it.
       You just pretend you don't.'

I couldn't tell him how ashamed I felt
because Daddy had just lost his job and already was sad.
He stayed home with my little sister and me while Mommy
worked in the evenings.

Besides, sometimes Daddy is bossy and mean and
I'm afraid of him."

LOVE said,
   "You can practice telling me
   what you wish you could tell your Mommy and Daddy . . .
   especially your Daddy.
   Someday I hope you will tell THEM how you feel."

And Annie said,
   "Oh, LOVE, I have tried to tell Mommy. Three times!
   But once when I said I didn't want
   to go camping with Daddy
   she said, 'Don't be silly.
   Daddy would be so hurt if you
   didn't go.' So I went.
   And I was the one who was hurt.

Why do I have to *tell* Mommy, LOVE?
Doesn't she know by looking at me?"

LOVE didn't talk a lot. Mostly LOVE listened.
LOVE spoke quietly in a whisper and said,

*"I can't hug you,
but I want to."*

And he hopped up
on Annie's shoulder
and rubbed his soft feathers
on her cheek.

Annie cried
giant tears
on his
soft white body.

Annie said,
"You are all white and clean.
If you really knew me
you wouldn't like me
because I am dirty.
Daddy said so.
And he's right.

Something is terribly wrong with me
that other children don't have wrong with them."

And LOVE said,
*"Little One,
Precious Annie,
you feel guilty not just because of what
your Daddy has done to you,
but because sometimes you enjoyed the special attention.*

*It's not your fault.
You are a child.
Of COURSE you want your Daddy's approval.
But you didn't want to be HURT!"*

It was very dark outside and rain was beginning to fall.
Annie needed protection and ran for cover against the hard wind.

For just one moment as she entered Grandma's house
Annie thought it was not such a safe place *inside,* either!

Annie went straight to her room.
She felt restless and her tummy hurt again.

She lay on her bed thinking,
> *I'M SO AFRAID.*
> *HOW CAN I STOP THIS?*
> *WHO WILL PROTECT ME?*

> *Maybe I should run away from home.*

LOVE was perched on the window sill.
He looked at her in his gentle way
and said,

> *"I know you don't have words
> to explain what
> has happened to you,
> but you can
> show me on your dolly
> if you like."*

And Annie did.
And LOVE cried.

When Mommy
was in the kitchen
she said she hated
working at the
hospital and wished
Daddy would
hurry up and find work.
She told Annie,
"Don't tell Daddy
I said that because
it will make
him angry and
he might go away.
We can't make it
without him."

Annie lay on her bed breathing
like a frightened rabbit
just thinking about what Daddy had done to her.

She even wet her bed now
and she hadn't done *that* for years.
Maybe it was because of the nightmares.

"Yeah, I bet that's it.
I wet my bed during the nightmares."

When she looked at LOVE he nodded and said,
"I believe what you have told me
about your Daddy is true.
I know you wouldn't lie
about something like that."

He continued,
"You didn't do anything wrong.
I'm glad you told me.
Later there may be other things
you will want
to talk about
when you are ready.

When you are ready, Little One.
When you are ready, I will listen."

Annie said,
   "When Daddy said, 'Don't tell,'
   I knew what he was doing was wrong.

   I began pretending I was asleep
   when he came to my room.
   We both knew I wasn't,
   but it made it easier."

                    LOVE said,
                       *"I know.
                          I know."*

The best part about talking to LOVE
was that he was never shocked, disgusted or upset by
what Annie told him.

If he *had* been, Annie would have felt *she* caused
those feelings, not her Daddy.

When the storm was over
Annie went alone to the tide pools.
It was a special place, but dangerous.
The rocks that surrounded the pools were slippery
and the pools quite deep. Annie knew she could be hurt.

Maybe if she fell
she would be punished
for being so bad.

While she was sitting on the rock,
LOVE hopped up close and said,

> *"What do you mean BAD, Annie?"*

And Annie said,
> "My Daddy is mean to me,
> but it's OK because I'm a bad girl.
>
> I made my Daddy do this.
> I wish I knew how to make him stop.
> If I'm good Daddy won't hurt me anymore."

LOVE said,

*"You may have done some wrong things, Annie,
but you did not cause this abuse.*

I know you feel you caused this, but you didn't.

*IT IS NOT YOUR FAULT
WHEN OTHERS
MAKE
WRONG
CHOICES."*

And LOVE said, *"What else are you thinking about, Annie?"*

"Well, once Mommy caught me touching my
private parts in the bathtub and she screamed,
       'Stop it!
       That's dirty!'

So then I told her that *DADDY* touched me there,
but she just looked mad and left me.

Sometimes Mommy is at home at night
when Daddy comes to my room.

WHY
   DOESN'T
      SHE
        STOP
          HIM?"

LOVE said,

"It is because Mommy is hurting too.
This is hard for you to understand now,
but it is true.

YOUR MOMMY DOES LOVE YOU!

She is just afraid of what Daddy will do
if she talks to him about this.

But, Annie,
You have the right to say, 'NO.'
Because you love your Daddy
it will be hard
but you can do it."

Annie wondered why Daddy didn't have any friends.
When they went to church he didn't talk to anybody.
She couldn't think of one person who was his friend.
He must be very shy and lonely, she thought.

And LOVE said,

> *"You are right, Annie,*
> *Daddy is hurting too.*
> *He hasn't been able*
> *to admit that he needs help,*
> *or he doesn't know where to find it."*

Annie cried
and said,

"LOVE, who can I trust?
Who will be on *MY* side?"

And LOVE said,

"The hardest job of all
will be learning
to trust again."

In the morning very early Annie tip-toed
out of the cottage and went down to the beach.
It was so peaceful and quiet except for the sounds
of the sea. The waves had washed the beach clean again.

Annie whispered,
        "If only I could feel clean."

It happened again last night.
She heard him coming down the hall to "tuck her in."
Daddy didn't bring presents anymore.
And he wasn't patient.
When Annie started to cry, he said sharply,
      "Be quiet.
        I need you.
        Don't cry."

And *that's* when Annie decided to tell!!
She jumped up and marched in to Mommy and said,

      "Daddy is hurting me
        and you just have to stop it *now.*"

At first Mommy screamed and cried
and yelled at Daddy.
It scared Annie.

But after a while she wrapped
her arms around Annie
and said,

      "It won't ever happen again."

And Annie knew it was the truth.

LOVE said,

     "Some abused children NEVER tell.
     You were very brave.
            I'M SO
                PROUD
                   OF YOU."

LOVE said,
    "I have something
       to tell you
       that is very important.

You feel like a little broken dolly now,
      and dirty
      and hurt
      and guilty
      and sad.

But there are many GOOD people
who will NEVER, NEVER hurt you.

You won't always feel like this.

And, Annie, something else—
      I love you.
      And I know all about you."

LOVE said,
  "Now I have something to tell you
  which will be very hard to hear.
  I wish there was another way,
  but there isn't.
  Annie, this is it:

      You will need to forgive your Daddy
      when you are able. If you don't,
      you will become a prisoner
      of your hate.

          It won't be easy
          and you will need to do it
          again and again, but
          someday, Annie,
          I hope you will
          see your Daddy as I see him,

  a precious child of God who has hurt you,
  and who needs help."

Dear Friend,

There is no place so potentially violent as home. It is sometimes a place of special betrayal because the child's guard is down. If you are abusing a child, please accept help.

If you are being abused, tell someone and keep telling until you get the help you need.

HERE ARE SOME GUIDELINES FOR HELPING A CHILD WHO HAS BEEN SEXUALLY ABUSED:

1. Remember, children don't have adult vocabularies to describe what is happening to them. Watch for non-verbal clues such as: nightmares, withdrawal or restlessness, school or home behavioral problems, bedwetting, fear of a particular person, unusual interest or knowledge of sexual matters, blood on underwear, masturbation.

2. Children protect themselves by blaming themselves when something is wrong. They believe their parents are good and they cannot blame people they trust.

3. After the sexual abuse ends the child may still be an emotional prisoner. Abuse requires coping throughout life to separate the confusion between sex and love.

4. If necessary, encourage the child to talk about the experience again and again.